Of Two Minds

Ned Fain, Private Investigator,
Book 3

A Hard-boiled Mystery

Sam Abbott

Sam Abbott

Of Two Minds: Ned Fain, Private Investigator, Book 3
Copyright © 2015 Liz Dodwell
www.lizdodwell.com

Print ISBN-10: 1939860253
Print ISBN-13: 978-1-939860-25-5

Published by Mix Books, LLC

Table of Contents

One

If there's one thing that I truly enjoy, it's driving my car on a country road, and if there's one thing that can make that even more enjoyable, it's driving my car on a country road with a beautiful girl riding along. And that's as far as I'm going with that analogy, so keep your thoughts to yourself!

For those of you who haven't been reading these accounts of what I laughingly call my "adventures," let me introduce myself. My name is Ned Fain, and I'm a private eye.

I used to be a lawyer. I did the whole law school thing, even went to Harvard, but then I got disillusioned with some of the things that lawyers were doing, so right after graduation I joined the Army. They were thrilled to get an actual Harvard Law grad, so they immediately gave me a commission to Lieutenant and assigned me to a JAG Office. Two months later, they decided they needed a prosecutor to work war crimes in Afghanistan, and off I went. I did two tours there, but the second one ended early when one of the Afghan officers I was prosecuting for atrocities hired someone to kill me.

A grenade got tossed into the latrine while I was taking a break, and it almost got the job done. I spent four months in the hospital, lost about half of my right foot, more than half of my hearing and suffered burns over a fair part of my body, including my face.

Yeah, I'm pretty ugly. Deal with it, I do.

They gave me a medal and an Honorable Discharge with a small pension, and sent me home, but I didn't really have one to go to. I ended up living in a flop hotel, one of those where you pay your rent by the week, and trying to find odd jobs to live on. See, I couldn't handle going into a court room, and the only law job I could find would be in a Public Defender's office. Every time I think about walking into a court room, I panic, though, so I gave up on law after about a month. I ran into an old friend who was painting houses, and he gave me work whenever he had it. I hated it, but it paid the bills and fed me.

Then I blundered into a murder scene, and the number one suspect happened to be a pretty school teacher who sold me on her innocence. She'd known I used to be a lawyer and tried to hire me, but I told her I couldn't help, that she needed a lawyer who could actually defend her. She then proposed that I work for her as an investigator, to try to prove that the victim's widow was a more likely killer than she was. I started to say no to that as well, but the ten grand she offered as a retainer made my head nod the other way.

Long story short, she turned out to be guilty, but would have gotten away with it if I hadn't figured that out. I managed to get her on tape confessing to the crime, and that was that.

I had actually liked the work, and I was still a licensed attorney and member of the BAR, so I spent some of that money on a PI license and opened up shop. Stumbled into a mess right after that, but it led to me catching a big time drug dealer that the feds had been after for years, and there was a hefty reward. I'd met a girl who was a computer whiz and helped me on that case, so I hired her as my secretary and assistant.

Yes, she's pretty, and she can stand looking at my ugly mug every day. Those aren't her most important qualities, but they sure don't hurt.

So now you're up to speed on Ned Fain, Private Eye; let's get back to this story.

On one particular night, not long after the events described above, Sylvi—that's the girl, my assistant—hinted that she wouldn't mind if I took her out to dinner. So I loaded her into my car and drove her over to Marquette, to a restaurant I'd heard about that was supposed to have really good steaks and seafood. We had a good time, flirted with each other a bit, which we do all the time (even though I know she isn't serious about it), and were on our way back to the city.

All of a sudden, this guy runs out in front of the car and froze like a deer when my lights hit him. I slammed on the brakes, and the guy turned and looked back the way he'd come. I got a brief look at his face, and then suddenly his face exploded, a split second before I heard the blast of a shotgun.

Sylvi screamed, and I skidded the car to a stop just a few feet from the dead man. I was out of the car in a flash, hoping he might still be alive, but that would require him to still have some of his brains, and there was almost nothing remaining above where his nose should have been. Pretty grisly, but I'd seen things like it before, so I kept my bile down and used a pen to flip his jacket open and look for ID.

Sylvi came out of the car to stand beside me, and I was impressed that she managed not to get sick and contaminate the scene. She had her phone out and had already dialed 911.

No wallet in the jacket; I felt his back pockets with the pen, and there was nothing there, either, nor in any other pocket. The guy's suit was a cheapo, off the rack job, but I noticed that the waistband of his underwear was marked "Tommy John," and they're about eighty bucks a pair. I wondered why a guy who could afford them would wear a Kmart Blue Light Special suit, but you just never know about people.

Sylvi said, "Cops are on the way. I said he was dead, but they're sending an ambulance, anyway."

"Standard procedure. They naturally assume that the person calling in is an idiot who wouldn't know dead from Denver." I stood up and looked into the woods in the direction the shot had come from, and it hit me that the killer might be aiming at us at that moment.

"I didn't see anyone," I said loudly, hoping that would satisfy the shooter, and Sylvi responded that she hadn't seen anyone, either.

"I heard a shot, sounded pretty loud. Did you hear it?" She knew about my hearing problems, and that my hearing aids didn't help all that much.

"Yeah. Shotgun, probably a twelve gauge loaded with double ought buckshot. That's like getting hit by a dozen bullets all at once, does this kind of damage."

I looked back down at the victim. He wasn't too old, maybe early thirties, and seemed to be in pretty good shape. What I could still see of his haircut looked like it was done by a pro, so that was another thing that wasn't cheap. I sniffed and smelled cologne.

Sylvie said, "Clive Chancetian," and I turned to look at her. "The cologne, you're sniffing it. I know it, it's Clive Chancetian's 1872."

"Expensive, right?"

She nodded. "About four hundred an ounce."

"How do you know all this crap?"

She smirked at me. "You haven't exactly been keeping me busy, you know. I surf the web a lot, and things just stick in my head." She shrugged. "Besides, my ex-boss wore that stuff all the time, and bragged about how much it cost. He was a jerk."

Expensive cologne, expensive hairstyle, expensive undies and a cheap suit. Something about this didn't smell right, but about then we heard a siren, and I remembered that it wasn't a case I was on. The locals arrived a minute later and took our statements — I didn't bother to tell them my conclusions, let them figure it out — and ten minutes later they let us go with the customary, "We'll call if we have any more questions!"

I drove Sylvi on home, and we didn't really talk a lot. She was looking out the window, and I think I heard a couple of sniffles. She's got a big heart, Sylvi does, and I think she cries for people who die with no one to care about them, or who die unfairly. I left her be.

Two

Okay, fast forward three months. I've got bills piling up on the desk, and while I've still got a fair chunk of change in the bank from the reward I got on the drug dealer, it's not gonna last forever, especially when I've got Sylvi to pay—and there is no way I'm letting her go! The few little jobs I've gotten lately were solved mostly through her ability to get into just about any database in the country, so she's indispensable.

Yeah, and she's a babe. So sue me for being male.

Anyway, while we're sitting there playing rummy, the little light went on that meant someone had walked in, and Sylvi turned to greet a woman. She was about thirty-ish, not too hard on the eyes, well dressed and obviously not hurting for money, from the clothes she was wearing.

"Hi, how can we help you?" Sylvi asked, and the woman smiled a little tensely.

"I'm—I think my husband is having an affair," she said.

I hate those kind of jobs, because they usually mean sitting in a car or somewhere for hours on end, doing nothing. They're boring, with a capital B.

On the other hand, it meant money coming in, and that's the whole point of being in business, right? I was thinking of how much to charge when Sylvi smiled up at the woman and said, "Our standard rate is a hundred and fifty dollars an hour, plus expenses, and we require a one thousand dollar retainer."

See? That's one more reason to keep her around, because the woman smiled again and said, "Yes, of course, that's fine," and took a wad of cash out of her big Gucci purse. She counted off ten hundred dollar bills into Sylvi's hand, and I invited her to take the chair across my desk.

"I'm Carolyn Cahoots," she said to me, "and I hate that it's come to this, but something has been different about Chance for a while, now, and I can't get him to tell me what's wrong. He just keeps saying it's nothing, but I know better. He went on a business trip a few months back, and when he returned it was like he was someone else. He'd lost a lot of weight, and he was just—I don't know, it was like he was irritable all the time. He..." she paused, and I sat there in silence, waiting for her to go on. If you're quiet for a moment, they always do.

"He hasn't touched me since he got back. The next day, he moved into a separate bedroom. He'd always been so attentive, before, and so I think he must have found someone else, and I just need to know."

I nodded sympathetically, which is something Sylvi taught me to do in situations like this. "Mrs. Cahoots, I understand, and I'm sorry you're going through this. I can promise you I'll get to the bottom of it as quickly as I can." Yeah, Sylvi taught me that line, too. "Tell me more about your husband, please?"

"Chance is a functional consultant for government-run educational institutions, like schools on military bases.

He works as an independent, travels a lot, sometimes abroad. He's good at what he does, he's always provided us with a good living, and that lets me do some of the volunteer work that I love."

"I see. Any children?"

She shook her head. "No; Chance never wanted any, I'm afraid."

"Okay. Have you seen any of the usual signs that indicate infidelity? Lipstick on the collar, unusual charges on your credit card bills, strange women calling, or someone hanging up when you answer?"

She shook her head again. "No, nothing like that. As I said, it's just that he's so different. An affair is the only thing I can think of."

"Would anyone else know much about what he's doing, or what he might be going through?"

This time she nodded. "His mother," she said. "He spends a lot of time with her, so she might know something, though she'd never tell me. We aren't exactly close."

I stood and said, "Let me get started on this, Mrs. Cahoots, and I'll try to have something for you within a few days. And, by the way, do you have a photo of your husband?"

She dug into the Gucci again and handed me a photo of her husband, Chance. It showed a man with nice hair, in good shape, and wearing glasses. "That was taken about two years ago, for business," she said. "He doesn't wear the glasses anymore, just contacts, and he's lost about thirty pounds, but other than that, he looks much the same."

Something about the guy looked familiar, but it could be that he just had one of those faces, or maybe he'd been on TV at some point. I didn't know him, but I'd know him a lot better than he knew himself in the next few days.

Mrs. Cahoots gave us a lot of his info: social security number, date of birth, facebook account and such, and then shook my hand and left. I told Sylvi to get on her computer and get me everything she could on the guy, while I paid a visit to his mommy.

The older Mrs. Cahoots, who went by the unfortunate name of Toots, lived in what used to be a servant's cottage on a big estate outside of the city. I found it with my phone's GPS app, and the Mustang got me there in about forty five minutes. I rang the doorbell, and a woman of about fifty-five answered.

"Can I help you?" she asked, and I showed her my ID.

"I'm Ned Fain, a private investigator, Ma'am, and I've been asked to look into some things that may be affecting your son, Chance? His wife is pretty worried about him." Never tell a mother her son is cheating on his wife. "I was wondering if I could ask you some questions."

She hesitated for a second, but then opened the door and invited me inside.

"Nice little place," I said, and she smiled as she led me to a sofa. I sat, and she sat on the other end.

"Yes, well, this used to be my gardener's place, back when we owned the estate. Unfortunately, my husband made some bad investments before he passed away, and the place was too expensive to keep up, so I sold it some years ago. I kept this part, with the garden and cottage, so I'd have a home."

I nodded. "How long have you been a widow?"

"Almost twenty years, now. Irvin died of a heart attack, and the death taxes were the final blow to our finances. Selling off let me have enough to live on for the rest of my life, but it hasn't been easy."

"I'm sure it hasn't. Mrs. Cahoots, could you tell me when you last talked to Chance?"

She blinked. "Oh, goodness, he calls me now and then, but I haven't seen him since before he went to wherever it was, a few months ago. He stays pretty busy, you know. And as for my daughter-in-law, she's prone to what we used to call the vapors; she tends to see a problem where none exists."

That was odd, Carolyn Cahoots had said that her husband visited his mother often, and the way she'd said it made it sound as if she considered it true. It was unlikely she'd believe that, unless she had reason, but his mother said he only called, and hadn't come by, lately.

I let that slide for the moment, and asked, "Can you think of any reason there might be problems between them?" She shook her head.

"The only problem I know of that they ever had is her spending faster than he was making, but that isn't the case anymore. Chance has been doing very well lately, so they aren't hurting for money at all. If you ask me, the only one there who might be a little strange is Carolyn, but that's just my opinion."

I didn't seem to be getting anywhere with her, so I thanked her and got up to leave. She went with me to the door, and as I stepped outside I noticed that the old family place was not visible from her house, because of a large brick wall that seemed to be new. It wasn't important, but I commented on it as I was saying goodbye.

"Yes, when I sold the place, the people who bought it were old friends, and they were always nice, you know; they'd come over and check on me now and then, and invite me up to the house for dinner, but they sold it again a few months ago, and the new owners put that up. I think they run some kind of private club there, now, but it doesn't matter to me. It always kind of hurt to go back and see it being lived in by others, you know?"

I told her I could understand that, and drove away. Another dead end, but that was the way cases like this usually went.

I went downtown to where Chance Cahoots had his office, and found his car in the parking lot of the building, took a spot close to it and watched. I could see the door of the building, as well as the car, and after a few minutes I even spotted Cahoots through his second floor window. I got out my Nikon digital camera and used the zoom feature to watch him as he talked on the phone and worked on a computer. I could actually see the monitor pretty well, and from what I saw, he wasn't using it to talk to anyone, just writing some kind of document.

I sat there for about three hours or so, and finally he came out. It was around four o'clock by then, so I figured he was getting off work for the day, and I tailed him from a distance to see where he might go. Imagine my surprise when he went straight home like a good boy.

I sat outside his condo building all evening, and when I caught myself dozing around eleven, I gave it up and went home. I live in the back room of my office, to save having to commute to work (and it's cheap), so I was still sacked out in the morning when Sylvi came in.

Three

We had a nice little arrangement, Sylvi and I. She was willing to let me open my eyes and look at her sexy little self in the mornings, so, in return, I allowed her to bring me coffee and breakfast (okay, doughnuts) and walk right into my room without knocking. It was a fair trade, if you ask me, even though I was paying for the coffee and doughnuts out of our petty cash box. I think she liked it, too, because she always wore clothes that looked sexy as all get out, even though no one could say she wasn't dressed decently.

Whatever; it certainly brightened up my mornings, and if she got a little thrill out of knowing I liked what I saw, that was okay. Some girls just have a need to tease a guy, and since I wasn't going to hit on her anyway, she knew teasing me was safe. At least, I think that's what she figured.

She'd already told me that she hadn't found anything in any of Cahoots's records, except that old man Cahoots had been named Irvin Nash – get it? I. N. Cahoots? She thought that was really funny. Anyway, I didn't expect her to have any new answers for me. Good thing, because she didn't. I threw off my blanket and went to get a shower while she opened up the office.

When I came out front, clean and dressed, Sylvi was at her desk. I sat down in mine, which was right behind hers and let me observe her from one of my favorite angles, sipped my coffee and ate one of the doughnuts she'd left on a paper towel for me. It tasted great, and I don't think that had anything to do with the view.

Okay, maybe it did, but who cares?

Sylvi was looking at pictures on her computer, and I realized she had downloaded them from my camera. I could see the one she had up on the screen, a picture of Chance that I'd snapped when he came out of his building, and got up to stand behind her.

"I'm telling you, I could swear I've seen that guy before," I said, and she shrugged.

"Doesn't look familiar to me. Maybe back in your lawyer days?"

I shook my head. "Maybe, but I doubt it. It'll hit me sooner or later. Let's look at the rest, see if you spot any sign of cheating."

She turned her head to look up at me. "Are you implying that I've been cheated on so much that I'd know a sign of cheating if I saw one?"

I glanced down and looked her over. I couldn't imagine that anyone who had her would ever give serious thought to having an affair. "Okay, guess not."

"Ha!" she barked in my face. "Of course I would! Men cheat, Ned, not because their woman is undesirable, but because they're wired that way. The hottest girl on earth has had a man cheat on her, or at least try to. The only reason a man ever stops cheating is when he's really, truly, absolutely in love! So let's see what we find in Mr. Cahoots, here!" She spun back to the monitor and started scanning through all the pictures.

A half hour later, she told me, "Sorry, Ned. From what I see, this guy is married more to his work than his wife. Maybe that's all that's wrong, he's just tired of the old ball and chain."

I didn't have a response, so I sat quietly and finished my coffee, then headed out. It was still only a little before seven, and I wanted to tail Cahoots from home.

I got to his street about ten minutes before he left, which was good for me, and followed him away from his place. He drove to a coffee shop and got a tall latte, then went on to his office. Big surprise.

I parked and waited. At lunchtime, he came out and drove to a small restaurant in an old part of the city, and I perked up. It was the kind of spot most people would choose for a secret lunch rendezvous, so I waited 'til he was inside, and then slipped in and sat at the counter. I could see him reflected in a mirror over the entrance to the restrooms, and out of the corner of my left eye. I ordered a ham and cheese on rye and watched.

He got a burger and fries, and the only person to join him was an old man of about sixty. I couldn't hear them very well, but the words I caught were about some school software that wasn't doing whatever the old guy wanted it to do.

They talked like old pals through lunch, and when they finished up I was already back in my car and waiting. Naturally, he went right back to the office, and my boring waiting game began its third round.

At quitting time, he drove straight home again, and I sat outside until ten. When nothing happened by then, I snuck out and placed a motion-activated mini-camera in a bush near his car, where it could snap pics of the building entrance and the car itself, and went home again.

Those little cameras were awesome. When Sylvi woke me the next morning, I told her about placing it and a few minutes later she had its view up on her computer. They were wired for the internet, and she could log onto some website, enter the ID for that camera and see whatever it had snapped pictures of all night long, or activate it and watch in real time. She scanned through its memory, and found nothing but a dog peeing on Cahoots's tire, and an old couple and some kids going in and out of the building. No sign of our suspected Lothario.

I sighed, and went back to watching him the old fashioned way. I left my camera where it was, so I wouldn't have to sit outside his place all evening, and followed him to work yet again.

He didn't go out for lunch that day, so I had to go without, but I always keep emergency rations in the glove box. Two bags of Cheezits were enough to carry me over, but when four o'clock came along, I knew I'd be ready for some food.

I didn't get to wait that long, though, because Cahoots came out at about one thirty and got into his car. Short day, I figured, so I followed him, expecting him to go home like always, but this time I got a surprise.

He got on the interstate, and I followed as he went out towards where his mother lived. I figured he was finally going to visit her, but stayed with him to be sure, and I'm glad I did. He didn't go to Momma's house; he turned in at the old family estate, instead.

I sat out of sight and watched through bushes as he showed the gate guard his ID and was waved on through. That was interesting, and I wondered what was going on in there, and what it had to do with Cahoots.

I called Sylvi. "Guess what?" I said, and she bit.

"What?"

"Cahoots just went into that fancy place that used to be the house he grew up in. I'm sitting outside now, watching, and the place has more security than Fort Knox."

"Really? That's intriguing," she said.

"Yeah. See what you can find out about who owns or runs the place. The address is..."

"I've got it. I'll check county property records now and get back to you."

"Good girl," I said.

"Of course I am," she said with a giggle, and hung up on me. Sometimes I think she flirted with me just to make sure I'd want to keep her around for daydream material. Other times, I wondered if she actually liked me, but then I'd wake up and get real again. Beautiful girls don't go for guys with mangled faces.

Or would they? You always see stories about some ugly guy who gets a beautiful girl, like in Beauty and the Beast. Could a girl like Sylvi ever really care for a guy like me? I didn't know, but it would be hard for me to believe. The only thing I knew for sure was this:

If I ever got Sylvi to look at me with the look of love in her eyes, the last thing I'd ever consider would be cheating on her. And if that meant that I was falling in love, then so be it. She'd never know, because I'd never take the chance that she'd decide working for me was too weird if I told her how I felt, so it was all a moot point, anyway.

Okay, no more daydreaming.

Four

I was parked on a high spot near some trees and bushes about a quarter mile from the place, and was watching through the zoom on the camera. One of the things I noticed was that there were a lot of expensive cars in the parking area, cars like Cahoots's Mercedes, but also more expensive ones like Bentleys, Jaguars and even a Maybach or two. Even us ex-lawyers know our luxury cars, and I confess to doing a bit of drooling over these. I jotted down a few of the license numbers and emailed them to Sylvi with a request to run them and see who owned the vehicles.

A delivery truck from some flower company pulled up to the gate, and the guard came out. I had a fleeting thought of renting a truck and trying to sneak in as a delivery guy, find out what was going on in there and what it had to do with Cahoots, but that fantasy crashed when the guard made the truck wait outside the gate. A golf cart came up, and three big guys transferred a whole load of some white flowers onto it, and then took them up to the house. I snapped pics of the flowers, and sent them to Sylvi as well.

Cahoots came out after about two hours, and I carefully tailed him back to his office. I can say the guy didn't act like he was worried about getting caught at anything, because he never even checked his rear view mirrors, just cruised along like he owned the road.

We got back to his office, and I parked in the lot where I usually did. He got out and went inside, just like always.

I sat there for about an hour, and suddenly Sylvi showed up. She climbed into the car, and I could have kissed her, because she brought me a couple of burgers and a big cup of coffee the way I like it. That girl is worth her weight in gold to me, and I'm not kidding about that!

She smiled at me as I chowed into the burgers, and said, "I got you some info. That place was bought by a company called Bai Mudan. It's owned by a trust, which is called The Bai Mudan Trust; big surprise, huh? Now, the problem is that I haven't been able to find any kind of corporate records, not for the company or the trust. I did a quick Google search and found out that Bai Mudan is a Chinese tea made from white peony flowers, and guess what kind of flowers those were that you took pictures of? You got it: white peonies."

I looked at Sylvi and shook my head. "Are you trying to tell me that this is some sort of private club for tea drinkers? That's nuts!"

She shrugged her shoulders at me and smiled. "Do you think it makes any sense to me? I think it's crazy, too."

I shrugged back. "And the big question to me is, what does this have to do with the husband?"

Sylvie shrugged again. "Maybe he's not really doing anything wrong, and this is just some sort of business club. I mean, stranger things have happened."

I sighed. "Maybe I should just tell the wife there's no evidence of any cheating, and drop this whole case."

Sylvie looked at me. "But something is telling you that there's more to this than meets the eye, and you're not ready to give it up yet, right?"

"Yeah, pretty much."

"So where do we go now?"

I nodded toward the fancy cars sitting in the parking lot, and asked if she had had any luck with tracing any of the license numbers I'd sent to her.

"Not yet, but I'll get on that as soon as I get back to the office. I thought you'd want this info—oh, and some lunch—right away. Right?"

"Of course you're right, and what would I do without you? I'll tell you what; why not just start on the license numbers in the morning, and take the rest of the evening to yourself. I'm pretty sure he's going to go straight home again, and the spy cam is already in place, so I'm going home to get some rest after I leave here."

She nodded. "Okay. I've got a yoga class I want to go to tonight, anyway. See you in the morning, Chief!" She got out and went to her little Scion out on the curb, and zipped off.

I waited 'til quitting time, and sure enough, he went home like he had each night, so I checked that the spy cam was still where I'd left it and did likewise. Getting home early was a treat; it meant I could have a microwave dinner and watch reruns of Supernatural on Netflix.

Supernatural is my favorite show, because it shows two guys who are willing to go up against impossible odds to fight evil, and no matter how bad it gets, they never back

Sam Abbott

down. Sam and Dean became my heroes the first time I saw the show, about a month after I got back from Afghanistan, and unless time just didn't permit, I tried to watch at least one episode a day.

That night I watched seven, back to back, before I passed out on the couch around midnight.

I woke up on my own, which was unusual. Sylvi hadn't come in and gotten me up, but when my eyes focused, I saw the big coffee sitting on the end table and smiled. I guess the TV had still been on when she came in, so she knew I'd been up late watching the guys and let me sleep in.

My phone said it was almost nine, but I was pretty sure I knew where my subject was, so I didn't panic. I showered and got dressed, then went out to the office.

Sylvi was on her computer and turned to smile at me. "Morning, Sunshine! I'm in the DMV database, and guess what?"

I took a big swig of coffee and said, "You found my long lost rich uncle?"

She shook her head. "Nope, but I did find out that almost all of the cars whose tags you got belong to various corporations, and some are rentals, but one of them is privately owned. That one belongs to a man named Harland Swafford, and he's about seventy five years old. Got his address right here." She passed me a sticky note with an address.

"Hmm. So whatever it is, it's not just for young guys like Cahoots. Something about this is just eating at me, you

28

know that? I think I'm going to go see Mr. Swafford and try to get myself invited to the club."

I punched the address into my phone and let it guide me to one of the ritziest apartment buildings in the city. The place had security and required a key card to get in, and with the video cameras all over the place, there was no way I was going to be able to slip in behind another tenant. I was sitting there wondering what to do when I spotted Swafford's car. It was the Maybach, the one I'd made goo goo eyes at, and it was coming out of the parking garage, so I fired up and moved to follow.

Five

He drove to a medical office building, the kind where a dozen different doctors share a front office. When he parked and went inside, I was quick enough to hold the door open for him.

This man may have been seventy five, but he looked about ninety! I wasn't a bit surprised to find him going to a doctor. Compared to how he looked, I could enter a beauty contest and win it! He signed in and sat down to wait.

A few minutes later, a nurse came out and called his name. I waited a few seconds before following and watched her lead him into a urologist's office, a fancy place. A receptionist looked up at me as I entered, but I just smiled and pointed at Swafford, and she grinned and went back to what she was doing. I walked over and took the seat next to the old geezer.

I glanced around to make sure no one was watching us, and then I leaned in close to him. He turned toward me, looking a bit startled, and I whispered, "Hello, Harland. We need to have a little chat about Bai Mudan."

His eyes shot wide open and his face went beet red in a split second, and I thought, Oh, Geez, I've given the old buzzard a heart attack! I leaned in again and added, "Get this straight—I'm your old buddy, Neil Fitz, and you like having me around to help you handle things. As soon as we get a minute, we'll talk, but don't mess this up!"

31

He nodded, and forced himself to get his face and breathing back under control. I could have sworn that he was terrified, and I wondered if he thought I was a cop or something like that. Maybe I'd stumbled onto something big, like the drug dealer a while back. I could stand another big reward like that!

A different nurse came out and called him in, and I got up to follow. The nurse held up a hand to block me, but I caught Swafford's eye.

"He's with me," he wheezed out. "An old friend." The nurse shrugged and led the way into the examination room, took all his vitals and then left us alone.

He looked at me, and I could tell he was scared. "What do you want? How much? I'll pay, I swear, just don't tell anyone, please! I'm begging you!"

I didn't have a clue what he was talking about, but I didn't want him to know that, not just yet.

"Calm down, Harland, your secret is safe with me, and so is your money. All I need is to get inside the Bai Mudan, and I want you to arrange it."

The old man stared at me. "Honestly?" he asked. "That's all, and then you'll leave me alone?"

"That's all. I just need to get a look at it from the inside, and no one will ever know that you helped me do that. You'll never hear from me again."

He looked at me, afraid to believe me but not daring to doubt. "Are you a policeman? I swear, if there's anything illegal going on, I know nothing. I only go for the services, nothing else, I swear. I'm a member, not one of the partners."

I smiled at him. "Okay, relax. All I need is for you to put me on the list as an invited guest."

He stared at me. "What is it you're hoping to find there? If this is about blackmail..."

I shook my head. "I just have my own reasons for wanting to know what that place is all about. For that, all I need is a chance to get inside and see with my own eyes, and that's all I need from you. The name is Neil Fitz, remember?"

He nodded vigorously. "Neil Fitz, yes. For when?"

I thought about it; both Swafford and Cahoots had gone in the daytime, so odds on that would be the best time to find out what was going on in there. I smiled and said, "How about tomorrow afternoon? That sounds like a good time to be there, doesn't it?"

He nodded. "Tomorrow afternoon, then. Let me make the arrangements." The old guy took out a smart phone that made mine look like a stone tablet, and whispered, "Bai Mudan," to it. A moment later, he said, "Mr. Jordan, this is Mr. Swafford. I have a friend coming by tomorrow afternoon who would like to sample your wares." He listened for a second, and then looked me pointedly in the eye. "Oh, of course I'll vouch for him, I've known him for years. His name is Neil Fitz, and you'll know him because of some scarring on his face." He listened again and then smiled. "Thank you, Mr. Jordan. I'm sure he'll find it to be everything he's looking for!"

He ended the call and looked at me, his smile gone completely. "You're in, Mr. Fitz. If you do anything there that reflects badly on me, I'll be ruined. I'm praying you're being honest with me, and that I won't be seeing you again."

I patted his shoulder again. "Mr. Swafford, your secret is safe with me; I have no reason to cause you any problems, and I promise you that I won't, unless something there goes terribly wrong. Since this is just a sight-seeing tour, I don't really think there's anything to worry about, though, so after we leave here, you'll be done with me."

He nodded. A moment later the doctor came in, and I stood by and acted like the concerned old friend as they discussed prostate problems and FlowMax dosages. When the appointment was over, Swafford actually thanked me for coming and asked me to walk him out to his car.

"Mr. Fitz," he said once we were outside and alone, "there is something about you that makes me trust you on this. I have no idea what it is you're looking for, but somehow, I hope you find it." We got to his car and he turned to look at me. "Should it happen that you need more from me, and on the condition that your motives are not criminal, I would not object to speaking with you again."

He handed me a business card that said, "Harland Swafford, Private Investments." I tucked it into a pocket and shook his hand.

"There's nothing criminal in my intent, sir," I said. "Thank you." I opened his door for him and helped him in, then shut it and watched him back out of his space before I went to get the Mustang.

Sylvi was delighted when I called to tell her I had gotten a way into Bai Mudan, and we started brainstorming on how I'd make the most of it. By the time I got back to the office, we'd decided to rent a limo and some fancy duds so I could give off the image we wanted, and Sylvi even found a place to rent a chauffeur's uniform, so she could be my driver.

I gotta say, she looked very hot in that outfit. It had shorts, rather than slacks, and they fit her so well that…

Never mind.

Six

We arrived at Bai Mudan at three, and the guard stepped out as we approached the gate, waving us to a stop

"Good evening," he said, and I leaned out the window I'd rolled down. 'How can I help you this afternoon?"

"Hello," I said crisply. "My name is Neil Fitz, and I'm a guest of Mr. Swafford."

The guard looked at my face closely, then scanned a list he held on a clipboard. He smiled.

"Yes, Mr. Fitz, I've got you right here. Please follow the yellow line on the drive to the parking area, and you'll see the guest entrance. There's a chauffeur's lounge there, where your driver can wait, and they have a juice bar and other amenities for them." He glanced at Sylvi. "I'm sure she'll be well entertained while she waits."

"Thank you," I said, and Sylvi drove through the gate as it opened. She was the perfect chauffeuse, hopping out to open my door for me, and pulling off an adorable British accent. As I stepped out of the car, I said, "I'll call when I'm ready, Hillary," and she snapped back with a perfect, "Veddy good, Sir, I shall be waiting."

That girl is a godsend! No matter what I ask of her, she's always ready to play the part and help me out. In this case, she'd also be listening for any gossip among the other drivers. There might not be any, if the place was so security conscious as it seemed to be, but if she heard anything she felt I should know, she'd tell me.

The guest entrance was under a portico, and a man in a tuxedo was waiting to open the door for me. He smiled as I stepped inside, and said, "Good evening, Mr. Fitz. I am Mr. Jordan, the director. I hope you enjoy your visit with us this afternoon." He held out his hand with a small package in it. I took it, thinking it had some sort of information or party favor inside, but what I pulled out was a soft, satiny mask.

I stared at it for a second, and then looked up at Jordan. I was about to tell him where he could shove his mask, thinking that it was some sort of insult about my scars, when he smiled and said, "The mask is optional, of course, but most of our guests do prefer to maintain anonymity, here. It's entirely up to you."

I caught myself just in time and thanked him, then put it on. It made sense; whatever it was about this place that made Swafford terrified of anyone finding out why he came, it would undoubtedly make others want to keep their involvements secret, especially from other guests. That explained why Swafford wondered if I was into blackmail, as well.

"In addition, most of our guests use pseudonyms; I've taken the liberty of calling you Mr. Torrance, I hope that's all right?"

"That's fine," I said, and he nodded and told me to follow him.

The house was huge, and we made our way down a long hallway into a bar area. The liquor was artfully arranged behind one of the most ornate bars I've ever seen, but the thing that caught my attention instantly was a set of red velvet-covered couches in the corner.

Okay, it wasn't the couches; it was the twelve almost naked women that were sitting on them. There were blondes, brunettes, redheads and some with so many colors I got dizzy. There were small girls and big girls and some that almost looked like men in drag, and I wouldn't have taken bets that they weren't!

Surrounding these women were men, and I saw that all of them were wearing masks like mine. Some of them went even further, wearing costumes of various sorts. I saw a gaudy, obviously fake General's uniform, a guy dressed up like a bear, and one that was wearing almost as little as the women, and with a horse's tail hanging off his bottom end! He even had a bridle on his face, and I suddenly got a very bad feeling about the place!

The bartender was a tall girl with blonde hair, and like all the others, she was dressed in what amounted to a leather thong bikini. She smiled at me as she asked what I'd like, and I hesitated.

I'd stopped drinking when I got into the PI business, but before that I'd been drunk a lot. I didn't want to get started again, and while I'd drunk mostly cheap beer, I knew that alcohol of any kind would be a bad idea.

"Virgin Mary," I said, and the girl didn't even bat an eye. She passed me my glass of spiced up tomato juice, with a stick of celery for a garnish, and I gathered that I wasn't the only teetotaler to patronize the place.

Mr. Jordan spoke. "If you'll follow me, Mr. Torrance, I'll show you around, and we can discuss the type of servicing you might be seeking." He led off down another hallway, and I followed.

We stopped at a door, and he opened it to let me look inside. I was suddenly very glad I was wearing the mask, because I'm sure my face would have revealed my shock. The room was a torture dungeon, and I'm not exaggerating! There were chains and manacles along one wall, and a rack held dozens of different kinds of whips, paddles, riding crops and other devices that I was sure were designed to deliver pain to someone! Over in one corner was a big X-shaped wooden device that was obviously designed to restrain someone. I didn't even want to think about what would be happening to the person so restrained, but I'd bet it wasn't about to be pleasant!

I looked it over and nodded, trying to give the impression that I was not surprised. He closed the door, and we moved to another one.

This one held a huge, circular bed, and the entire room was covered in mirrors. There were mirrors on every wall, and the ceiling was one huge mirror. I was suddenly reminded of an old Dean Martin movie about Matt Helm, a secret agent who made James Bond look like a prude! He'd had a bedroom like that in one of his movies, and I recalled that when I'd seen it (I think I was about fourteen), I'd thought it was cool. Looking at this one made me feel dirty.

Jordan closed the door and we walked on. As we walked, he said, "Many of our guests enjoy simple spanking, some on the giving end, and others on the receiving. Some prefer more intricate fantasies, of course, such as role playing, or pony or puppy play. May I ask your own preferences?"

Okay, here's where my experiences in Afghanistan came in handy. One of the cases I had to prosecute was an American captain who had set up a sort of club along these lines for his fellows, using local women who were forced to participate. In that case, I had to learn quite a lot about the BDSM lifestyle, which was something this captain had been into even before his military days. He'd found that a lot of his fellow officers liked it, too, which is not surprising since it's all about control. By coercing women into serving as submissives or slaves, he had a roaring little business going, until one of his clients was arrested for beating a woman to death. The whole story came out, and it was a sad chapter in our presence there.

Now that knowledge came to my rescue.

"I'm a dominant, myself, and mostly into the physical aspects, rather than the fantasies. My friend told me I might find some interesting situations here, so I wanted to check it out."

"I'm certain you will," he said, as he opened another door.

This room had an assortment of different clothing, most of it feminine and the kind of thing you'd expect to see a little girl wearing. There was a twin bed with a frilly canopy, and it didn't take a lot of imagination to figure out the sort of thing that went on in here. I swallowed my bile and smiled.

"Not my cup of tea," I said, and Mr. Jordan nodded with a smile and moved to open yet another door.

This room was occupied, and I would have probably backed out quickly but for one thing: There was a nearly nude woman, in the leather bikini that they all wore, holding a leash that was attached to a collar worn by a completely naked man. She was using a thin rod to whip his rear, yelling at him and calling him a "bad dog!" He was whimpering like a dog as she did so, but when the door fully opened, they both froze and looked at us.

Jordan muttered an apology and yanked the door shut, but in that split second of shock, I saw that the man being whipped was none other than Chance Cahoots. Even more than that, the look of utter surprise on his face made me remember where I'd seen him before.

That was the same face I had seen blasted off the man on the road, three months ago. That man had looked exactly like Chance Cahoots, and had worn that same look of shock and surprise, just before his face was obliterated by buckshot.

Jordan apologized to me for his mistake in exposing a client, but it gave me the break I was looking for. I drew myself up with all the anger I could muster—which wasn't hard, considering some of the things I'd seen in that place— and looked him in the eye.

"Mr. Jordan," I said as coldly as I could, "if you can make a mistake like that when you're showing a visitor around, then I'm afraid I would not be comfortable that you could preserve my own privacy. I'll thank you to forget that I was ever here. Would you show me out, please?"

"Oh, but Mr. Torrance," he began, but I shook my head.

"I'm sorry, I'd like to go."

He surrendered and led me back to the guest entrance. I handed him my mask, stepped outside and saw Sylvi standing beside the car, sipping a bottle of grape juice, and she spotted me at the same time. As I got to the car, she opened my door and held it as I entered, then got behind the wheel.

Seven

We didn't speak until we were off the grounds.

"So what's the big secret in there?" Sylvi asked, and I sat there for a long moment, trying to gather my thoughts and decide just how to tell her what I'd seen. I was still so shocked by some of it that I wanted to let it settle.

"I'll tell you when we get back to the office," I said. "It's too much to talk about while you're driving, you'd wreck the car and kill us both!"

She tried to get more out of me, but I refused to say a word until we got to my place. We had dropped her car off at the rental place, so she'd take the limo back in the morning; that left us free to go inside and talk it all over. I led her back into my room, and looked in my mini-fridge, wishing for the first time in four months that I had a beer. I settled for the root beer I'd taken up since then, and sat on the couch beside Sylvi.

"Do you know anything about BDSM?" I asked her, and her eyes went wide.

"Um," she said, "a little..."

"Well, five minutes in that place, and you'd know a lot more than you ever want to! It's a fantasy club, where people go to play those kind of games. They showed me rooms for spanking fantasies, master and slave stuff, even rooms full of dolls and toys, and I don't even want to think about what goes on in there! It was all I could do not to come running out of there with my hands in the air, screaming bloody murder!"

Sylvi sat perfectly still for about three seconds, and then burst out laughing like an idiot!

"Omigod," she said between gasps for breath, "as tough as you are, I can't believe something like kinky sex could make you panic and want to run! Ned, have you led that sheltered a life? I learned about all that stuff in college! You can't be a college student today without getting into some kinks, now and then!"

I glared at her. "It's not funny, Sylvi," I said, but that only made her laugh harder. I sat back in frustration and waited for her to run down. It took a few minutes, and finally she cleared her throat and said, "Okay, I'm good, now. So, what else happened?"

I looked at her, embarrassed to admit that I'd been so uncomfortable, but finally I just blurted out, "One of the rooms they showed me wasn't empty; Cahoots was in there, naked as a newborn and wearing a dog collar, while some woman was using a stick to whip his butt, and telling him he was a bad dog!"

That set off another round of uncontrollable laughter that was so bad she fell off the couch and onto the floor, and I threw my hands in the air and waited for her to get done again. It took another ten minutes before she managed to talk.

"Well, I guess we know why he isn't into the wife any more," she said, and then had to stifle another chuckle or two.

I nodded weakly. "Maybe; if she isn't into his games that might explain it. But there's something else that's really bothering me, and I don't have a clue what it means."

She sobered instantly; Sylvi knew me fairly well by then, and could tell when I was getting my teeth into something. "Spit it out, Ned," she said.

I gathered my thoughts for a moment, then said, "Remember a few months ago, that guy in the road that got killed?"

She nodded. "Yeah. Pretty hard to forget."

I looked her dead in the eye so she'd know I was being very serious. "I saw that guy's face, and you know I don't forget anything. When I saw Cahoots's face up close like that, and he was looking scared because we'd walked in on his kinky game, it hit me why he looks so familiar; it was the exact same face I saw get blown off that man in the road."

Sylvi sat there in silence. "What?" I said.

"Ned, you only saw that guy for a second before he got shot. Maybe there were some similarities, but it can't possibly be the same guy, he was dead!"

I shook my head. "One of the things you learn as a prosecutor is how to take in all the evidence and embed it in your mind. After a while, you get to the point that everything you see, everything you hear, it all gets embedded in your memory, and when you need it, you can call it up and look it over again. Seeing Cahoots with that same expression on his face, that 'oh, crap, I'm caught,' look, I suddenly saw the dead guy's face in my mind, and it was exactly the same."

Sylvi sat there for another moment. "Okay, well, I know you well enough to know you wouldn't say it unless you were certain, but I can't figure any way it fits in, can you?"

"Nope. Not a clue."

"Okay. Then we keep it in mind, but unless we see how it figures into Cahoots or the case, we just go on, right?" I nodded. "Good. Now, while I was waiting for you at the limo, I did a little research on my iPad, and found something that does fit. Remember I told you that Bai Mudan means White Peony? That's why they call the tea Bai Mudan; but I found out there is another reference to it, as well. Bai Mudan, or White Peony, was the name of a famous prostitute in Chinese history! Apparently she was considered the most beautiful woman who ever lived, and would give her clients any fantasy they desired, as long as they flattered her properly. I guess that means as long as they paid well."

I shook my head. "I didn't get a price, but I'm sure it would have been pretty well up there." I sighed. "I guess we've gotten to the bottom of our client's case, though. If Cahoots wants to be a pooch, maybe his wife can buy him a doghouse and collar and save the marriage. Assuming she'd want to, that is. We'll talk to her tomorrow. I know we've gone over the retainer, so get her bill ready in the morning."

She nodded. "Okay. I'll see you then," she said and rose, but then she looked over her shoulder at me and I could smell the mischief rising in her. "Unless you want me to stay and spank you?"

I think my eyebrows bumped the ceiling. "Any spanking that goes on between you and me is going to leave your tail end sore, not mine, and I'm too old for you, so get going! I'll see you in the morning!"

She laughed and headed out the door, pausing just long enough to say, "You never know, you might be missing out on something you'd love!"

"Git!" I yelled, and she got.

Eight

Here's some advice for anyone who has an employee that is overly familiar with you: fire them!

I woke like a shot the next morning, because Sylvi snuck into my room, set my coffee on the coffee table and then smacked my rear end as hard as she could before running into the front office. I came up off the couch and almost chased her down, before I realized I was in my boxers.

"That," I yelled, "will be the only time you ever do that!" I stomped into my bathroom and took a shower to cool myself off. And no, just for the record, it did NOT turn me on. It might have made me think about returning the favor, though, but I didn't have time for things like that.

When I came out to the front office with my coffee, Sylvi was on the phone, talking to Mrs. Cahoots.

"Okay," I heard her say, "we'll see you then." She hung up and turned to face me. "Sorry about that, but after last night, I just couldn't resist. I won't do that again."

"Darn right, you won't," I said.

"Okay, Mrs. C. will be here in an hour. I didn't give her any information, just said you needed to talk to her about the case. Oh, and I did your hours, and her bill is on your desk. You've got about eighteen hundred coming."

"Good, we need it! Let's get this place tidied up a bit before she gets here."

We busied ourselves for a few minutes picking up pop bottles and paper cups, then Sylvi even dusted off our desks and the credenza she'd made me buy. By the time the client arrived, the office looked pretty nice.

Sylvi met her at the door and seated her at my desk, then asked if she wanted coffee or anything, but she declined.

"I just want to know what's going on," she said nervously, so I cut to the chase.

"Mrs. Cahoots," I said as gently as I could, "I'm afraid I found that your husband has gotten into some things that may be upsetting to you. Have you ever heard of a place called Bai Mudan?"

I was surprised when she nodded. "Yes, that's the club that bought his family's old estate. I don't know much about them, I'm afraid."

"Well, they are a very private club that caters to some very specific needs of their members. In this case, I'm afraid your husband has been going there to..." I swallowed. "He goes there to explore a fantasy about being treated like a dog, and getting spanked or whipped."

She froze solid, and didn't even blink. For a second, I wondered if I'd given her a stroke, but then she took a deep breath.

"Oh, my god," she said. "Oh, no. I've been worried he might go mad, but nothing like this ever even crossed my mind!"

I squinted. "Why did you think he might go mad, Mrs. Cahoots?"

She looked at me as if I should already know the answer. "Well, his brother. His twin brother went crazy when they were boys, and was institutionalized for trying to kill Chance when they were fifteen."

Something went click in my head, and my heart started pounding. "Were they fraternal twins, or identical?" I asked her.

"Oh, they were identical, that's why I was worried about it affecting him, too. I never met Cole, that was the twin's name, because he died from some kind of accident at the institution a few years after he was put there. Chance never talks about him, but his mother has mentioned him a few times." She looked at me, as if about to share a secret. "I think she has a few issues, too, because Chance says she's never accepted his brother's death. She still talks about him as if he's alive, and even used to talk about going to go visit him sometimes."

I let all of this roll through my mind, and then I heard myself say, "Okay, that's fine. Now, I've still got a few things to look into, if that's okay, and we'll have your bill for you in a couple of days. I hope this information helps you in some way, and if I get anything else, I'll call you right away."

She thanked me profusely and then left, and Sylvi came to sit on the edge of my desk.

"Twin brother, huh? You get the feeling the twin wasn't dead, after all?"

"Oh, he's dead, all right, but it wasn't as long ago as she's been told. He died three months ago, on a road not all that far from where his mother lives. What bothers me is why this woman doesn't know that. Didn't the cops ever identify the body?"

Sylvi shrugged, but said, "I'll find out. Give me a little time to get into the right databases."

"Okay. I'm gonna go see Momma Cahoots again. Something isn't adding up, and you know how I hate that!"

"Yeah," she said, "about the way I hate a toothache!"

I headed out the door and got into the Mustang, then drove back out to the cottage where Toots mother lived. I was almost there when Sylvi called.

"Get this," she said. "John Doe's body was never identified, because his fingerprints were not on file. They didn't bother to check dental records or DNA because they didn't have a missing person report that matched. So with no one to claim the body, he was buried in the local Potter's Field with no headstone."

Potter's Field is what cemeteries call the plots they donate to the homeless and indigent; it comes from the Bible, the field that Judas bought with the silver he was paid for betraying Jesus. He killed himself there, and it became the place to bury the poor who had no grave of their own.

"Wow," I said. "What a world we live in. Okay, check one more thing for me..." I told her what I wanted to know, and she said she'd get right on it.

Toots seemed surprised to see me again, and a bit nervous, but she let me in.

"Ma'am, I just learned about your son's twin brother, and I'd like to know more about him. Can you fill me in?"

"Oh," she said, "why, yes. Cole and Chance were identical twins, you know, so identical that we couldn't ever tell them apart. I used to dress them differently, put one in red and one in blue, that sort of thing, so I'd know which was which; but the scamps would sometimes switch on me, playing games. They were wonderful boys, just mischievous, you know? At least, until they got older."

"What do you mean?" I asked.

She looked a bit sad, then, as if what she was about to say would somehow hurt her. "When they got into their teens," she said, "they just seemed to grow apart. They'd always been close up to then, but suddenly one of them was the good student, and the other wouldn't even try. Chance was always the good one, though Cole would always claim that wasn't true and complained he was getting the blamd for the stuff Chance was doing. There were problems at school, Cole trying to touch some of the girls inappropriately and things like that; I got called in more than once. Cole always swore that it wasn't him, but the girls were sure because of what he was wearing. Then, when they were fourteen, we came home one day to find our dog dead on the front porch. He'd been gutted and hung up from the awning, it was horrible. Chance swore that Cole did it, and I found a bloody knife hidden in one of Cole's desk drawers. That was almost the last straw, but Cole swore he'd behave, so I didn't do anything about it." She let out a long sigh.

"Then, a year later, the boys got into an argument. Cole attacked Chance with a hunting knife and almost stabbed him, but Chance managed to fight him off, and Cole ran. Chance chased him, and by the time I got there, Cole was down on the ground, bleeding from his head. Chance said Cole had fallen and hit his head on a rock, and we couldn't wake him. An ambulance came, and they took him to the hospital. He was in a coma for about three days, and when he woke up he couldn't even remember what had happened. He had some brain damage, the doctors said, and a pretty serious memory loss, but the worst part was his anger. He'd get so frustrated at not being able to remember things, he'd just explode for no reason at all, and we finally had to agree to put him in a special hospital. I used to go and visit him, but it always seemed to upset him, so finally I stopped going except for once or twice a year."

I felt sorry for her, but I wanted answers, and this was no time to play nice. I asked the question I had prepared in my head before I got there. "How long ago was it that he died, Mrs. Cahoots?" I asked, and she looked at me strangely.

"Died? He didn't die; in fact, he was released a few months ago. He'd been undergoing some experimental treatments, and they'd been very successful, so the hospital released him. He showed up here to visit, and we had a wonderful time!"

Nine

I was taken aback, positive that my bad hearing had failed me again. I had been watching her lips, and I knew what she'd said, even if I found it impossible to believe. "You knew all along that he was alive?" I asked. "Carolyn said Chance told her he died in an accident in the institution."

She waved a hand in disgust. "That one," she said, dismissing her daughter in law as if she were no one important. "Why, yes, of course he's alive! He came by when he was released, and we had a terrific visit. I called Chance to let him know so he could come and see him, too. Cole stayed here for about a month, and then decided he wanted to get out and be on his own."

"Chance knew he was here?" I asked, and she lowered her eyes.

"I just said that, didn't I? In fact, to be honest, that was when he told Carolyn that he was going to China or wherever, but he was really right here, visiting with us. The two of them were getting along so well, and it felt so good to have them both here with me again. They'd go out and spend the day together, and come back with dinner for all of us. It was a wonderful time."

"So what happened? How did it end?"

"Cole decided he wanted a life of his own, you know. They went out one night and talked, and Chance gave him some money and helped him find a job doing some kind of writing—he was always good at that sort of thing—and he went out to California. He calls now and then, just to let me know he's okay."

I sat there for a few moments, trying to figure this out. There was no doubt in my mind that one of the twins was dead, but which one? I decided it was time to play my ace in the hole.

"Mrs. Cahoots," I said, letting a bit of steel come into my voice. "What are you going to say when I tell you that I saw one of your sons get killed a few months ago?"

She looked up at me instantly, and I saw that while she hadn't expected the question, it hadn't come as a complete surprise, either. "What?" she asked, trying to look startled. "What do you mean? Cole is fine!"

I grinned, knowing I had her. "Mrs. Cahoots, I didn't say it was Cole I saw killed, but you already knew it had to be him. It happened on the Marquette Road, about three miles from this spot. He ran out in front of my car in the middle of the night, but before I could stop and find out why, he was shot in the face by a shotgun that took most of his head off. The killer was gone by the time I stopped, and there was nothing I could do for your son, so I called the police and let them handle it."

She sat there for a moment, and I could tell she was trying to figure out what to say to cover her own rear, and then tears began to fall.

"I didn't know," she said, "but I'll confess I've wondered. When I get the calls, it's always from a blocked number, and I wondered if maybe it was Chance. He just sounds different somehow." She let out another deep sigh.

"When it happened," I said, "your son was wearing a cheap suit, but he had on expensive underwear and a very expensive cologne. His hair was done up pretty professionally, too, and I know that isn't cheap. Any idea why he'd have been dressed in such a fashion?"

She nodded. "Yes. When he was released, they gave him a suit to wear, but as you say, it was from some discount store. Chance took him out to be groomed. I'm sure he got him the cologne, as well, but I guess they never got around to buying new clothes." She sighed. "I confess I'd wondered if something had happened to Cole. When he decided to leave, he didn't come back and tell me, just called on the phone. He didn't even pack his things, they're all still in his room."

I felt anger rising; no one should die alone and unwanted. "And you didn't think it important enough to come forward? I just found out that your son is buried in a pauper's grave not far from here, and no one even knew his name."

She looked back at me, and there was a bit of fire in her eyes. "And what would you have had me do? Accuse my other son, the only one I've got left, of killing him? I don't know for sure that's what happened, Mr. Fain, and even if it did, I have no proof! If Chance killed Cole, then it's because there was bad blood between them, and a lot of it. I'm sorry, and I did love both my sons, but Cole caused us a great deal of heartache! Those aren't the kinds of things you ever get over, not completely, and I'm sure that there must have been more that I didn't even know about. Chance was the one who stayed out of trouble, who went to college and became a good husband and provider. If he had some resentment toward his brother that made them enemies, I can't say I don't understand. I had my own share of grief from Cole, you know. Their father's death was around the same time as when Cole went into the hospital, and I'm sure knowing the truth behind it was part of the reason Irvin took his own..." She stopped suddenly. "I don't want to discuss this any further, Mr. Fain. And I think that I would like you to leave, now."

I shook my head, disgusted. Maybe I'd feel differently if I had sons of my own, but I doubted it. Murder is murder, no matter who does it, and no matter who the victim is. I can't say there aren't some times when it isn't justified, and even necessary, and I've been one to make that call, myself; but there was something about this case that just rubbed me the wrong way.

I left, and as I got into the car, a thought struck me; Carolyn Cahoots was going to confront her husband about his kinky little excursions, and I'd just become convinced that the man was a killer. Suddenly I was worried for her safety, and dialed her number.

No answer. I called Sylvi.

"Yeah, Chief"

"Sylvi, Momma Cahoots says Cole was released from the hospital months ago, and Chance lied about his trip overseas. Instead he spent time with her and his brother. I'm pretty sure that he killed Cole, and that means he's not afraid to commit murder. If Carolyn tells Chance what I found out, she could be in danger! Try to reach her and warn her, and get the cops on it, too. Call Detective Mulcahy and tell him I'm about to hand him another murder case. I'm on the way to Cahoots's place, now."

"Got it!" she said. "And look at your email; I dug up what you asked about, and you were right!"

I thanked her and hung up, then gave the Mustang's big engine enough throttle to leave black marks on the highway, even though I was already doing sixty. Sylvi called me back to say that Mulcahy was going to "look into it," and I filled her in on everything else I'd learned from Toots. After I'd told her the whole conversation, I hung up, pushed the car for all it was worth and hit one twenty on some of the long, straight stretches, and fishtailed around all the corners. I got to Cahoots's condo building in less than twenty minutes; ahead of the cops.

I rang the buzzer, but there was no answer. I was trying to figure out what to do when a woman came out, and I forced my way past her and into the building, then ran through the hall and up the stairs to their unit.

My bad foot does not like it when I run, but it's learned that there are times when I won't let it have any say. This was one of those times; it was screaming when I got to the third floor, but I didn't care.

As I got to the door, I heard shouting, and then a scream. I tried the door handle, sure it would be locked, but it turned and opened, and there in front of me was a scene I never want to see again. Cahoots had his wife held by one arm around her throat, and a butcher knife pressed to her jugular.

"HEY!" I yelled as I ran inside, and she grabbed the distraction and bit his arm like a rottweiler! He let out a screech and let her go, the knife flailing away from her for a moment, and she ducked out of his grasp just as I got hold of his collar and dragged him back from her.

"Heel, Fido," I yelled, but I think that only set him off worse, because he whirled at me and swung the knife for my face. I've got all the scars there I need, thank you, so I pulled back, and that turned out to be a good move. He followed, and the more I fell back, the more he came after me. Stumbling backward was another of those things my foot hated, and it began yammering at me almost immediately, but I kept going anyway. Cahoots kept coming after me, too. I could see his wife, cowering on the floor behind him, but she had a phone in her hand, and I hoped she was calling for help!

I shouldn't have let my attention slip, because another swipe of that knife caught me on my right arm. It hurt like mad, and I yelped, but Chance didn't slow down a bit.

I continued to try to fall back, drawing him out and toward the hallway, but he got lucky again and caught my left shoulder with the tip of the blade. It stabbed in, not too deeply, and I actually fell as I tried to pull away from it. I hit the floor, my foot screaming in protest as it got twisted under me for a moment, and the madman advanced with a look like pure glee on his face, ready to finish me off and get back to what he'd been doing when I interrupted.

He lunged at me, ready to bring the knife down into my heart, but I wasn't out, yet. I remembered when Sylvi had been down, her hands and feet bound, while the Electric Axeman was trying to kill us both. She'd swung her feet in around his and clamped his legs between her thighs and calves, so I rolled and did the same. When I continued rolling, it brought him down onto the floor, facing upward, and I got to my knees and punched him in the throat as hard as I could.

My shoulder was screaming from the stab wound, but I put everything I had into it anyway, and it left him gasping for breath. I got up on my feet and kicked the knife away, just as three cops came rushing in with Sylvi right behind, telling one of them that he could take his order to stay back and shove it up his…

Yeah, that's Sylvi.

Ten

My old pal, Detective Mulcahy, showed up and kind of took over then. Carolyn explained that she'd hired me to find out what her husband was up to, and that when she confronted him about the Bai Mudan club, he'd gone nuts. He'd told her that she had no right to interfere with his life, and when she'd tried to tell him she cared about him and was worried, he'd told her that she was just like his mother, always claiming to care about him, but it was really just his twin brother that everyone loved! He had lost all connection with reality at that point, and that's when he tried to stab her. She'd fought him off for a few minutes, and I'd come in just as he was getting the upper hand.

Mulcahy turned to me and gestured at the man in cuffs on the floor. "So, this is really the twin who was institutionalized, right? Your girl filled us in on that part, and I guess that explains why he seemed so different, right?"

"Can't be," I said, and they all looked at me. I pointed at Cahoots. "This is Chance, the real one. And he killed his brother, Cole, who was locked up in a mental institution for years."

"How do you figure that?" asked Mulcahy.

"Simple enough; Cole had no fingerprints on record because he'd been locked up in a private institution all his life, but there are prints for Chance, because he has government contracts. So if it had been Chance who was shot, you'd have been able to ID him easily. Your John Doe had no records; therefore, the dead guy is Cole, not Chance.

"When Cole got out, released because he was successfully treated with some new therapies, he came home, and at first his twin was glad to see him. My guess is that Chance soon got fed up with Momma gushing over her poor little boy who was finally back with her. Sort of like the prodigal son story in the Bible; the one who'd always been there was jealous of the one who'd been gone and come back. After a while, Chance got so jealous that he decided to kill his brother. Momma pretended not to know what was going on, but she'd guessed that the son phoning her these past months was really Chance, pretending to be Cole."

Sylvi said, "Then, maybe Chance was the real bad twin, all along. Maybe Cole was telling the truth when he said he was being framed for all that stuff."

I shook my head. "I don't think so," I said. "I don't think there was just one of them who was bad; I think they both were, but maybe in different ways. Some kinds of cruelty are related to hereditary conditions, and when we dug into things, we found that old man Cahoots actually killed himself after being implicated in the rape and murder of a teenage girl."

Mulcahy nodded, as though I was making sense, but then looked at me again with that questioning expression of his. "How do you figure Chance killed his brother? I mean, how did he set it up and pull it off?"

"Mulcahy, that's your job. If you want my guess, I'd say Chance took Cole out for a ride in the night, then stopped the car and ordered him out. He took a shotgun out of the trunk or back seat, and Cole took off running. When he ran in front of my car he panicked and froze. That gave Chance the chance to fire, and run away while I was trying to find out if the victim was alive."

Mulcahy agreed that there was enough evidence to arrest Chance not only for the attempted murder of his wife, but assuming the body that would be exhumed from the potter's field turned out to be his brother, for murder, as well. Chance was taken into custody, his wife was taken to the hospital and treated for minor injuries and shock, and I went to the ER with Sylvi to get a few stitches of my own.

While we were in the ER, Sylvi asked me, "So, where did the kinky club fit into all this?"

"Near as I can tell, it doesn't, not really. It was just the place where Chance went to get his jollies. I figure he found out about it while he was staying with his mom and Cole, and talked his way into a membership. But to be honest, if we hadn't been suspicious about it, he'd probably have gotten away with murder. If I hadn't seen him in a vulnerable spot, naked and being whipped, he'd never have looked enough like his brother for me to make the connection to the dead man in the road."

She shook her head. "This was by far the weirdest case, yet," she said, "but knowing you, something will come along and replace it sooner or later. I can't wait to see what that might be!"

The docs came in and stitched up my little injuries, told me to take it easy for a few days, and let me go. Sylvi drove me back to Cahoots's place to get my car, and then followed me home, but I told her I was tired and just wanted to rest.

She smiled. "Tell Sam and Dean hello for me," she said, and drove off to her own place.

Morning came, and I woke to find her standing over me, holding a big cup of coffee. I reached up and took it, and threw off my covers. I was wearing a pair of shorts and a T-shirt, so I just followed her out to the office. We got there just as the mailman came in and dropped another pile of envelopes on her desk.

"More bills," I said, and Sylvi nodded, so we began going through them. She wrote out the checks and I signed them. That occupied us for a couple of hours, and then we spent a couple more writing up all my notes on the case. I tended to leave that for the last thing to do, since I kept it all in my head, anyway.

We were sitting around about noon, wondering what to order for lunch, when the door opened. We looked up to see Carolyn Cahoots come in.

"Mr. Fain," she said, "I just wanted to come by and thank you for saving my life last night. I'm not entirely sure how I'm going to get through all of this. Chance has confessed to the whole thing, and his mother was arrested last night as an accessory to murder, and also confessed. The whole thing is just a shock."

I nodded. "I'm sure it is," I said, "and I wish it hadn't been so crazy, but I think you'll be okay. Just take it one day at a time; I know from experience that's the best way to handle anything traumatic."

She smiled. "Of course. And I wanted to settle my account with you, as well," she said, and pulled a check out of her purse. "I know you didn't give me my bill yet, but I think this should cover it."

The check was for ten grand, and I looked up at her with my eyes wide.

"Consider it a bonus, Mr. Fain. With Chance's confession, I have been given full access to all of our bank accounts, and it seems he's been holding out on me. We have several million dollars that he made from some software patents or something, and I never knew until you came along. It's my way of saying thank you."

She smiled once more and walked out, and I thought that she wasn't going to have too much trouble adjusting to life without Chance. A few million dollars can be a wonderful form of therapy, I was sure.

A moment later, my phone rang, and I answered it to hear Detective Mulcahy yelling at someone in the background. I said, "Hello? Hello," and finally he spoke to me.

"Ned? It's Mick Mulcahy. Listen, we just raided this Bai Mudan outfit, and I wanted to let you know I appreciate the tip off on it. This is gonna be one of the biggest prostitution busts this city's ever seen, and it's all mine!"

I smiled. Mulcahy can be a pain, but he comes through in a pinch, and he's fair about giving credit where it's due. "My pleasure, Mick," I said, using his nickname for the first time. "Good for you!"

I heard the noise in the background go down, and I think he covered his mouthpiece. "I owe you one, Ned. And I don't forget. Let me know when I can do you a favor, okay?"

"You got it, and thanks," I said, and we hung up. Sylvi was standing there with a "what gives" expression, so I told her about what he'd said. She looked at me for a second, and then her eyes went wide.

"Oh," Sylvi said, "I forgot!" She ran out the door and to her car, returning a moment later with a planter full of flowers. They were white, and I stared.

"Don't tell me," I said, shaking my head, but she giggled.

"Yep! White Peonies!"

She set it in the front window, right under the sign that identified my office.

The end.

If you enjoyed this story, please leave a review. Your words really mean a lot.

Get a FREE *unpublished* Ned Fain story and be among the first to hear about Sam's new book releases and special deals when you join his email list here:

http://www.mix-booksonline.com/sam-abbott-insiders

Get more adventures with tough, sometimes cynical private eye, Ned Fain for one low price:

Ned Fain Private Investigator Series: Books 1 - 6

And see all of Ned's books here:
http://www.mix-booksonline.com/category/sam-abbott

Sam Abbott

Sam Abbott

…is a pseudonym for a popular author of adventure and cozy mystery. Who is that, you ask? Well, that's another mystery.

Join Sam on his facebook page:
https://www.facebook.com/SamAbbottAuthor

If you enjoyed this book, you might like:

- Adventure/Mystery – **The Captain Finn Treasure Mysteries:**
  - o The Mystery of the One-Armed Man
  - o Black Bart is Dead
  - o The Gold Doubloon Mystery
  - o The Game's a Foot
- Adventure/Mystery – **The Agency Confidential series:**
  - o Deceit
  - o Cheat